Cascade had drawn his gun, so there was paperwork for that as well. He had to explain why he had drawn his gun and what he was thinking and everything.

Then he still had the task of checking in Eve's body, which took even more time.

He kept hoping Eve was still around, but she never touched him to let him know if she was or wasn't and he didn't hear her voice.

When she had been inside him, he had realized that when he started hearing her voice, she was actually naked in the back seat of his patrol car. That thought just made him smile.

Finally, he managed to get out of the hospital and down to headquarters where he had to spend even more time filling out paperwork there.

He didn't mind the paperwork when it meant he had saved a life. And thanks to Eve, this evening he had.

Now, somehow, he just hoped Eve was still around.

And then, as he was heading for his car to go home, she touched him.

And he could feel her and her presence was with him and that just made him smile once again.

The Ghost of a Chance Series

(READING ORDER)

Though these books can be read in any order as they are all stand alone stories, this is the order in which they were written:

The Poker Chip: A Ghost of a Chance Novel

The Christmas Gift: A Ghost of a Chance Novel

The Free Meal: A Ghost of a Chance Novel

The Cop Car: A Ghost of a Chance Novella

The Deep Sunset: A Ghost of a Chance Novel

Also by Dean Wesley Smith

THE POKER BOY UNIVERSE

Ghost of a Chance

The Poker Chip: A Ghost of a Chance Novel

The Christmas Gift: A Ghost of a Chance Novel

The Free Meal: A Ghost of a Chance Novel

The Cop Car: A Ghost of a Chance Novella

The Deep Sunset: A Ghost of a Chance Novel

Poker Boy

The Slots of Saturn: A Poker Boy Novel

They're Back: A Poker Boy Short Novel

Luck Be Ladies: A Poker Boy Collection

Playing a Hunch: A Poker Boy Collection

A Poker Boy Christmas: A Poker Boy Collection

Marble Grant

The First Year: A Marble Grant Novel

Time for Cool Madness: Six Crazy Marble Grant Stories

Pakhet Jones

The Big Tom: A Packet Jones Short Novel

Big Eyes: A Packet Jones Short Novel

~

THUNDER MOUNTAIN

Thunder Mountain

Monumental Summit

Avalanche Creek

The Edwards Mansion

Lake Roosevelt

Warm Springs

Melody Ridge

Grapevine Springs

The Idanha Hotel

The Taft Ranch

Tombstone Canyon

Dry Creek Crossing

Hot Springs Meadow

Green Valley

~

The Cop Car: A Ghost of a Chance Novel

Copyright © 2016 by Dean Wesley Smith

First published in Smith's Monthly #23, WMG Publishing, August 2015

Published by WMG Publishing

Cover and Layout copyright © 2024 by WMG Publishing

Cover design by Stephanie Writt | WMG Publishing

Cover Art Designed by Lost Souls Studio

ISBN-13 (trade paperback): 978-1-56146-987-1

ISBN-13 (hardcover): 978-1-56146-988-8

The Cop Car

A GHOST OF A CHANCE NOVEL

DEAN WESLEY SMITH

WMG
PUBLISHING

For Kris
Long live popcorn for the brain

The Cop Car

PART ONE

A Ghost, A Cop, and A Really Good Meal

One

EVE BRYSON DIED so fast, she didn't even realize she was dead for a few minutes.

The rain was pounding down hard, one of those storms that felt more like standing under a cold shower. She had on only a light cotton summer dress, sandals, and panties. No bra, so this rain was sticking her dress to her like a second skin. Not pleasant in the slightest.

Around her the heavy pine forest seemed frighteningly dark, even though the sun was hours from setting. She could hear nothing but the pounding rain against her head, matting her long brown hair into a mess down her back.

She wasn't even sure how she had ended up in the rain. A moment before she had been driving toward a dinner date at a local brewpub in downtown Portland with three friends from college.

In the years since college, the four of them had managed

to get together every month or so and she loved those evenings. It took her mind off her worthless husband and even more worthless job she couldn't figure out how to get out of.

She had thought she would love high-tech work after coming out of college with her masters in engineering. But she hated it, hated the people more than anything else. Their goal wasn't to create new things, use their brains for good. All they did was try to figure out how to get ahead in the corporate game.

And just like her job, she thought marrying Simpson Jones right out of college was a good idea as well. It didn't matter that he was taking a break from finishing his degree. They had had great sex, lots of fun traveling, and planning for a future. She thought she had found a soul mate.

Maybe a soul mate for her single lost sock. But that might be giving Simpson more credit than he deserved.

It seemed good ol' Simp to his friends never understood that working was required to get ahead. She had no idea what he did all day while she was working, but it certainly wasn't anything to bring in money. She had a hunch he just looked at porn and played online games. She had gotten tired of asking about six months ago.

The marriage was that dead.

So for two years now she had supported him and that was going to end very, very soon. All of the rebel things she had found charming with him in college now just annoyed her beyond belief.

And all of her friends didn't like him either right from the start. That should have been a clue to her, but when a girl was in the first blush of love and sexual satisfaction, thinking with the logical brain wasn't that possible.

So she had made two mistakes right out of college. In six months, she would be out of both mistakes.

She shivered from the pounding cold rain and looked around. What had happened?

The two-lane winding road through the trees was empty. Water ran down one side, it was raining so hard.

Then she saw her wonderful little classic blue Miata off the road and down an embankment. Then she remembered. She had been thinking about how Simpson had complained that she wouldn't cook his dinner before she left. She had gotten so angry, she had been driving far too fast down the twisting area through the trees from their house in the hills to the main street below.

Far too fast for a pounding June rain.

She had slid into one corner, managed to get straightened out, and then didn't make the next corner. The last thing she remembered was the Miata heading over the bank and for a large pine tree.

She must have bumped her head. She didn't remember climbing up here to the road.

She quickly felt her forehead, looking for any sign of blood in the rain pounding at her.

Nothing.

The Miata's lights were still on and she went to the edge of the road to look down at it. It was pretty smashed up, but it wasn't that far off the road and the next person to come by would certainly see it and her.

She felt really sad she had totaled her Miata. She had bought it right out of college as well and it was the only fun thing left in her life after two years. Now it looked like she would be starting over completely.

The rain kept pounding at her and she could feel she was starting to really get chilled. It had been a seventy-degree day today. How could she be this cold?

A blue pickup, brand new from the looks of it, came around the corner, saw the lights from her car and quickly braked and pulled over onto the gravel shoulder of the road, putting on its flashing red warning lights.

The driver was a guy about forty. Maybe older. She could never tell with men in that range.

He pulled on a rain jacket with a hood as he climbed out and went to the edge of the road to look at her poor car.

She put one arm across her chest to cover what was showing through her wet dress and said to the guy, "I sure made a mess of it, didn't I?"

He said nothing, but instead quickly scrambled down the bank. When he got to the Miata, he looked inside, then shook his head and at a fast climb came back up the bank and started toward his truck.

"Why are you ignoring me?" Eve asked.

She reached for the guy as he went past and her hand went right through his arm.

And as it did, she could feel and read his mind.

All he was thinking was to get help out here quickly. And

that he doubted the woman in the car was alive. Her neck was badly twisted in a way that necks didn't twist.

She watched him move to the truck and climb in and use his cell phone to call for help.

Then in the pounding rain, she moved over to the edge of the bank and once again looked at her car.

She could see now that she was still inside.

She was dead.

And she was just about as cold and wet as she could ever remember being. And she was getting hungry.

She was dead.

She was a ghost.

How the hell could she be hungry?

Two

DEPUTY MCCALL CASCADE flat hated this part of his job. For two years now he had been working as a deputy sheriff. Except for the paperwork, he liked the job.

And he was good at it, actually.

But going to fatality crash sites was not anything he liked to do. Why would he? There was no one left to help.

He eased his patrol car over to the side of the road, but about four car lengths from the actual crash site since an ambulance was already taking up a part of that area. He turned on his lights to warn drivers coming down the winding hill.

He had also set flares back up the road. This road didn't have that much traffic, but in this pouring rain, he could see why someone would go off the road if not paying attention or driving too fast for the wet, slick pavement.

He pulled up the hood on his rain slicker against the hard, pouring and damned cold rain and climbed out, leaving his car running to stay warm and for all the computer equipment to keep running. Joining the force two years ago, he had been surprised at the amount of computer work they had to do.

He moved down to where the two ambulance attendants in yellow rain slickers were already going down to the wreck. He went over the edge to join them.

It was an instant verdict by both attendants. The young woman driving the blue Miata had died instantly on impact.

Cascade decided he didn't need to look. He didn't need the image in his mind. He had become a cop to help people, not stare at dead bodies.

He had the attendants get her purse and put it in a plastic bag. Then he headed back up the embankment to where the man who had reported the accident stood.

"She's dead, isn't she?" the man asked.

Cascade nodded.

"Damn," the guy said, shaking his head.

Cascade agreed with that completely. Thankfully she had been the only one in the car.

Cascade took the guy's name and address and thanked him for calling in the crash. Then he let the guy go, noting his license plate on his blue truck as the guy drove away.

Then Cascade turned to head back to his car and to find out the identity of the poor young woman in the mangled car below. It was going to take a while for all the angles of the accident to be photographed and her body removed from the car. Thankfully, none of that was his job.

He got back into his warm patrol car and dug out the woman's purse from the plastic bag, then her wallet inside the purse, and then her driver's license.

He sort of jerked as he saw her picture. She had been very attractive, with long brown hair, brown eyes, and a really nice smile that made her eyes seem to almost sparkle.

And she was his age.

"Too damn young," he said out loud, feeling a wave of sadness wash over him.

In the back of his mind he thought he heard a woman's voice say "Thanks."

He glanced around and then shook his head and pushed down his hood on his slicker and logged the information into his computer. This was just a tragedy, a horrible tragedy that there was no way he could have prevented.

A moment later he heard a woman's voice say in the distance, "Holy shit, someone who actually cares."

He again glanced around, but there was no one, of course. Maybe this was another of his superpowers that he didn't know much about.

He had agreed to become a superhero in the law enforcement division of the world. It seemed that everything that existed had a god around it and there were lots of superheroes around in most areas to try to help people.

He had no idea at all what becoming a superhero meant, other than she said he would no longer age and his natural talents would become more pronounced as time went on and he got control of his powers.

He had no idea he had powers. But he had to admit, he

saw things other cops didn't notice and he could almost read a person's emotions.

Reanna, his boss in the law enforcement side of super-heroes, had told him he had lots of time to learn.

He just wasn't sure what he was supposed to be learning.

And sitting in front of a tragedy where a young person died far too early in life sure wasn't teaching him anything. That he was sure about.

He shook his head and started to get out of the patrol car when he heard the voice again.

"Mr. Perfect."

He ignored it and closed the door and went back to help with getting the young woman's body out of the car.

He didn't feel like Mr. Perfect.

In fact, far, far from it at the moment.

Three

AFTER STARING AT her car for a moment in the pouring rain, Eve had managed to find a tree on the inside of the road to give herself some shelter from the rain. But by the time the first cop arrived, she had been shivering so bad, she doubted she could even walk.

Was it possible to die twice, once from a car crash, another from freezing to death?

One of the county sheriffs left his car running when he climbed out in his rain slicker. So she had gone over to his car and tried to open the backseat car door, but her hand went right through it.

"Shit!" she had shouted into the rain. "Just shit."

She needed to do something, so she closed her eyes and just pretended she was going to climb into the back seat. She wouldn't have been surprised if she had ended up sitting on the concrete, but she actually ended up in the back seat of the car.

Success.

She could go through a door, but not fall through a seat. Who knew?

And thankfully, the sheriff had the heater running on defrost to keep the windows clear, so it was warm in the car.

He had a towel beside his seat and she had grabbed it, coming away with what felt like a towel in her hands, but the original towel remained in position. The one in her hand looked identical.

She hadn't cared. Ghost towel or not, it was a towel.

Since she was a ghost, she had figured no one could see her, so she had stripped off her soaked dress and underwear and used the towel to dry off. Then she had finally used the towel to wrap up her wet hair on the top of her head.

She twisted the water out of her underwear and slid them under her butt to protect herself a little from the cold seat.

Then she twisted as much water out of her dress that she could and draped it over the front passenger seat to dry.

She was finally starting to warm up. She was naked and sitting in the back of a cop car. Under any other circumstances than being dead, this might have caused nightmares.

It still might.

The evening was just getting started.

Suddenly, the cop climbed back into his car. He was holding her purse in a plastic bag and as she watched, he pulled out her purse, then her wallet, then her driver's license and shook his head.

"Too damn young."

"Thanks," she said from the back seat.

He pushed his raincoat hood off the back of his head and she gasped. Sheriff man was about her age and a looker, with short brown hair, a square chin, and from what she saw in the rearview mirror, bright green eyes.

And she instantly noticed he wasn't wearing a ring.

What the hell was wrong with her? She was dead and lusting after a cop?

She stared at him for a moment as he called in her personal information and then keyed into the keyboard even more information, running her driver's license through a scanner.

She was impressed. One high-tech car.

Then he just sat waiting for even more information to come up on his computer screen.

She really wanted to know more about this guy. Dead or not, a girl could look, couldn't she?

Maybe if she touched him, she could read his mind like she had done with the guy who found her wreck.

She reached forward and put her hand on his shoulder.

Only her hand went inside him and she instantly felt the sadness he was feeling at her death.

"Holy shit, someone who actually cares," she said aloud.

He glanced around, making her pull back and cover herself.

Then he shook his head and went back to studying the information coming through her screen.

"Can I make someone hear me if I am touching them? How cool would that be?"

He didn't turn around at that, so she reached forward and once again put her hand inside his shoulder.

This time she let herself try to find out who he was before saying anything.

His name was Deputy McCall Cascade. Everyone just called him Cascade.

She liked that name.

He was exactly her age at twenty-six, liked his job except for events like this. He liked helping people and he didn't have a girlfriend.

But there was even more. He really worked as a superhero in the law enforcement area under a woman who was a low-level god in law enforcement by the name of Reanna. She reported to some gods above her, but he had never met any of them.

She had no idea what the superhero thinking was. Some sort of game or something. He was new at it, only being recruited by the gods of law enforcement two years before right after he had joined the force.

"Mr. Perfect," she said aloud with her hand still in his shoulder.

She could tell he had heard that.

He shook his head, put up his raincoat hood and climbed back out into the rain as another sheriff's car arrived followed by a second ambulance.

Wow, she was worth two ambulances. Thankfully she wouldn't be paying the bill on this one.

She watched for the next thirty minutes as they got her body out of the car and up into the second ambulance.

The more she sat there, the more puzzled she got by all of this. She had no idea what was going on.

She had never believed in ghosts or an afterlife or anything. But clearly she was living, at least for the moment, some sort of afterlife.

And she was hungry and pretty soon would need to pee.

You would think a ghost wouldn't have to deal with all the real world stuff. Rules of ghostieness were sure different from anything she had ever read or watched in the movies.

Twenty minutes later, Cascade climbed back into the patrol car and again lowered the hood on his raincoat.

Her breath caught, if she had been breathing, which she was pretty certain she had been. He had gotten even more handsome, if that was possible.

He moved her purse in its plastic bag from the console beside him to the passenger seat, then waited until the ambulance in front of him pulled away. He pulled out to follow it. It seemed he had gotten the duty of staying with her body.

If she had been alive, he could have done more to her body than just stay with it.

Then she laughed.

If he could actually see her in the back seat, sitting nude on her still damp panties, wouldn't he be surprised?

Actually, come to think of it, she was the one sitting here that was surprised.

She had expected a great night with friends.

She hadn't expected to die.

But she supposed no one expected to die.

She actually wasn't that upset about it for some reason. But she really needed to pee.

Four

CASCADE DROVE BEHIND the ambulance as they worked their way down the dark, tree-lined canyon and to one of the main roads. Neither he nor the ambulance had emergency lights on since there was no reason to be in a hurry.

Eve Bryson was in the ambulance and there was no doubt she was dead.

He just couldn't take his mind off the smiling picture of Eve on her driver's license. He had a sense that if he had known her, he would have liked her. Of course, that wouldn't have mattered since she was married and he never allowed himself to get near any married woman.

Actually, in the last few years, he had only dated a few times. He liked his solitude, mostly. And just hadn't found anyone that really attracted him.

Or that he felt a connection with in any form.

Eve's picture had attracted him, and he had felt an attraction to her. But maybe that was because she was safe.

She was dead.

And he had no idea where the voice was coming from he was hearing. That had never happened before. He was going to have to ask Reanna about that next time he talked with her. He wasn't certain if hearing voices was a superpower or a sign he was going crazy.

He didn't feel crazy. And the woman's voice in his head sure sounded sane as well.

Anything was possible, he was starting to learn. As a regular Marine and then four years of college, he had had no idea about any of this superpower and superhero stuff. No regular person did.

And now that he was starting to learn about it, he sure didn't talk about it to anyone. They would lock him away and toss the key into the brush.

That was another reason he hadn't found anyone to really care about. Supposedly he was going to live a long time. How could he tell a partner that he was a superhero and got his instructions from the gods of law enforcement? Not the best grounds for any kind of relationship.

He pulled into an area off the back of the hospital behind the ambulance. Damn he hated this. But it needed to be done.

As the two ambulance attendants got out and went to unload Eve's body, Cascade sighed.

He picked up her purse and his clipboard and ignoring

the woman's voice in his head talking about regret, he got out
to follow the body into the hospital.

He wanted to rescue people. Stop bad guys.

Not follow dead people around.

Parts of this job most certainly sucked.

Five

EVE HAD NO idea why the ambulance took her body to a hospital. She was clearly dead and they weren't even bothering to run with lights.

So as they pulled into a hospital loading area, she touched Deputy Cascade again.

The answer she was looking for came easily. Because she died alone and under suspicious circumstances, they had to do an autopsy. And it seemed in this county, the hospital morgue was where that was done.

"You won't find anything in my bloodstream except anger and a lot of regret."

She could see in his mind that he heard her. He wasn't certain what he was hearing, but he clearly heard what she had said.

He picked up her purse and she grabbed her dress. They

were parked under a canopy so she wouldn't get wet. She closed her eyes and pretended to open the door and step out of the back seat of the car.

The evening air had a chill to it and she was in front of a hospital, naked except for sandals on her feet and a towel wrapped on her head. Not this was the stuff of nightmares.

She quickly slipped her still-damp dress over her head. That sent shivers down her spine. But it was better than walking around a hospital completely naked.

Slightly better.

If there were other ghosts, she was going to make a great first impression. A dress you could see through and a towel on her head.

Cascade was striding toward the big double doors, following the gurney with her body on it.

She ran and caught up to him, going through the wide sliding-glass door beside him. Inside, the dim hallway smelled of antiseptic and roses, of all things.

The gurney with her body on it sort of clicked going down the smooth tile floor and she walked beside Cascade.

She just felt right walking beside him. Weird, but true.

In this part of the hospital, there sure weren't a lot of people.

But as her body turned to the right toward a service elevator, Cascade turned left and went through two swinging doors and out into a much more active and brighter area of the hospital.

Nurses and doctors were moving around, along with

patients and guests. Cascade seemed to know where he was going with her purse and the paperwork on his clipboard, so she just tagged along, trying to stay out of everyone's way, since none of them could see her.

And she almost succeeded in that task except for one man who came around a corner carrying a dozen roses. He had a dark look to his eyes and wore jeans, a T-shirt, and tennis shoes.

She went right through him before she really saw him.

And as she did, she saw why he was here.

His name was Jack Nevada and he was headed for a room she and Cascade had passed down the hall. Hidden in the roses he had a syringe that he was going to inject in a woman by the name of Stephanie to kill her. It would look like a natural death.

He was a paid killer, hired by Stephanie's husband.

"Holy shit!"

Eve froze in the hallway, watching Jack Nevada stroll toward his murder victim.

"What the hell! What the hell! What the hell!"

No one heard her.

What could she do? She was a ghost. She couldn't shout or even try to stop the guy.

She glanced back in the other direction.

Deputy Cascade, gun and all, had stopped at the nurse's station and was smiling at a young nurse in front of him.

Eve had to tell him, somehow.

She ran toward Cascade, her sandals slapping on the tile.

She tried to stop before she got to him, but instead slid and went right inside him.

He stood up straight as she did.

She liked it inside the big tall hunk of a man.

"Hi, handsome," she said. "Eve Bryson here inside you in ghost form. We got a problem that you need to solve real quick!"

He nodded to the nurse and stepped back, which made Eve smile. Even under stress of hearing voices, he could stay cool. This guy really was a superhero.

"I am, actually," he said out loud.

Some guy in a white smock looked at him and frowned.

"No need to talk in your out loud voice," she said. "I can hear everything you are thinking."

She felt him panic and she laughed.

"Yes, even the fact that you thought I was hot. Thank you, by the way."

He took a deep breath.

"So what do you need?" he thought at her.

She described the guy she had touched and what room he was headed toward and what he was about to do."

"Shit!" he said, again out loud. "Are you sure?"

"One hundred percent," she said to him. "And if you want to save that woman's life you had better get this handsome hunk of a body moving."

Damn, this ghost thing was getting better and better by the moment if she could be inside other people.

He touched the counter in front of the nurse. "Security to room 1003. Stat!"

He turned and started at a run toward the room, using his mike attached to his collar to call for backup of real police.

When he reached the room, he drew his gun.

She sent him calming thoughts.

"Thanks," he said.

Then he went inside, gun drawn, leaving the door standing open for backup to come in behind him.

The killer had put the roses down near the window and had a syringe in his right hand. He was working with the woman's IV and in another fifteen seconds would have injected her.

Eve had given Cascade a clear image of who the man was and what he was planning.

The woman under the blanket was a very large woman. And the room smelled like she had had an accident in the sheets.

"Step back and drop the syringe and put your hands in the air!" Cascade said.

Cascade's power and authority in his voice gave Eve little goose bumps. He could order her around like that any time he wanted.

"Trying to work here," he said in his silent voice.

"Sorry," she said, laughing. "Forgot where I was."

The man with the syringe looked shocked at the deputy and gun facing him.

The man took a step back.

"No worry," she said to Cascade. "He's not armed with anything but the needle."

"I said drop the needle and put your hands on your head."

The guy finally realized he had no options, so he dropped the syringe with a light click on the tile, then raised his hands.

At that moment two hospital security men came through the door.

"Needle on the floor," Cascade said to the security. "He was about to inject this woman with it. Hired kill I'm betting."

Cascade handed one of the security men his handcuffs. "Secure his hands behind his back."

The security man did and Cascade had the would-be killer sit on the floor with his back against a wall.

Then one of the security men used a tissue to pick up the syringe.

At that point, two police officers came through the door and the shit-smelling room got real crowded real quick.

"You're going to be busy," Eve said to Cascade. "I'm going to leave you for a bit."

"You coming back?" he asked in his inside voice.

"I think so," she said. "But I'm still new at this ghost stuff."

"So where are you going?"

"You don't know?" she asked.

"Not a clue."

"I've really got to pee."

"Ghosts pee?" he asked.

"I'm going to find out for the first time very, very shortly," she said.

And with that she stepped out of his body.

She felt almost empty not being with him.

She worked her way out of the room to find a woman's rest room. She doubted the hospital had ghost rest rooms.

But who knew.

Six

CASCADE FELT MORE alone than he had ever felt in his life without Eve's spirit or ghost or whatever inside him. She had filled parts of him he hadn't known were missing.

And now he had to suck it up and take on the business of being a sheriff.

First, he had to be in the poor woman's smelly room while everything was photographed and he walked through what had happened.

He had said he had caught a glimpse of the syringe in the roses when he passed the man walking in, decided it could be nothing but bad.

Eve had suggested that story before she left him to find a bathroom, since he pretty much couldn't tell anyone he had a ghost inside him helping him.

And since he had drawn his gun, there was paperwork for

that as well. He had to explain why he had drawn his gun and what he was thinking and everything.

Then he still had the task of checking in Eve's body, which took even more time.

He kept hoping Eve was still around, but she never touched him to let him know if she was or wasn't and he didn't hear her voice.

When she had been inside him, he had realized that when he started hearing her voice, she was actually naked in the back seat of his patrol car. That thought just made him smile.

Finally, he managed to get out of the hospital and down to headquarters where he had to spend even more time filling out paperwork there.

He didn't mind the paperwork when it meant he had saved a life. And thanks to Eve, this evening he had.

Now, somehow, he just hoped Eve was still around.

And then, as he was heading for his car to go home, she touched him.

And he could feel her and her presence was with him and that just made him smile once again.

Seven

I T TOOK DEPUTY Cascade two hours to fill out the paperwork on Eve's body and on the arrest at the hospital.

She had raided a candy machine for a few snacks by just sticking her hand through the glass and pulling out the ghost equivalent of a candy bar. The two bars helped a little to hold back the hunger, but she was going to need a real meal pretty soon.

Amazing how two candy bars could taste so damned good. Sort of like that first lick from an ice cream cone combined with the first bite into a perfect steak.

Heavenly.

Cascade then had to spend another thirty minutes at his desk at the police station filling out more paperwork before he could get off work. Wow did cops have a lot of paperwork or what? She had no idea.

DEAN WESLEY SMITH

She just sat off to one side and watched, admiring his wonderful body and handsome face.

She was a ghost, yet she had needed to pee and clearly now needed to eat. What rule said she couldn't lust after a live cop?

So as Cascade finally stood and started for his patrol car, she got back inside him.

"How you doing?"

"I was wondering if you were still here."

She could tell that he had missed her. As much as she had missed him.

This was getting interesting.

"Been watching the entire time," she said. "I figured if I was inside your body, I would just be a distraction to all the stuff you needed to get done."

"More than likely yes," he said.

And she could tell he appreciated that, even though he had missed her.

"Dinner at Shari's," she said.

"Ghosts eat and pee?"

"It seems we do," Eve said, laughing. "I need to eat because I'm ravished and the two wonderful candy bars won't hold me much longer. I died on my way to meet friends for dinner."

"I am so sorry to hear that," he said, suddenly feeling very sad.

"For some reason I'm not," she said.

So fifteen minutes later they were in Shari's restaurant.

This Shari's was like any other Shari's restaurant. Maroon

cloth and wood tones and lots of booths with tall wood walls between them. The place was known for great pies and they always had them in cases as you walked in.

Eve had just wanted to stick her hand inside one of the cases and grab pie and shove it in her mouth. That was how hungry she was. Somehow she managed to not do that, acting as if she was alive and following Cascade to a booth in the back next to a window.

She sat across the booth from him so she could see him, but she put her feet up so that they were in his lap, so she could be inside his head and he could hear her.

She told him how she was sitting.

"Kind of forward, don't you think?" he said, smiling.

Damn from across the table, she loved that smile.

"Thank you," he said, hearing her thought about his smile.

Then as the waitress came up, he ordered his regular French Dip and fries and a glass of iced tea.

"I'm going to go get something," she said. "Back in a moment."

She wandered into the kitchen and there, sitting under the light ready to take out, was a wonderful chicken fried steak meal. It smelled heavenly.

She picked up the plate, feeling the heat on her fingers.

The real plate just stayed there under the light. It seemed food had a ghost component as well, just as the candy bars did in the machine.

She took the plate back out to the table, put her foot against his leg and said, "I have chicken fried steak. So pardon me if you get moaning sensations as I eat. I'm that hungry."

She took a couple of bites, then realized while she was gone, he had called for his boss on the superhero side.

Just as Eve realized that, a striking black-haired woman in a police uniform came up to the table. She had to stand a good six feet tall and her uniform looked like it had actually been starched.

The woman nodded in Eve's direction and then had Cascade scoot over.

Eve moved so she could keep her foot in contact with Cascade.

"This is Reanna," Cascade thought at her.

"Figured as much," Eve said between bites.

This had to be the absolute best-tasting chicken fried steak she had ever had. Ever.

"I understand you just died this afternoon," Reanna said out loud to Eve. "Sorry for your loss, but glad you could help Deputy Cascade."

"Tell her it was my pleasure," Eve said out loud. "Ask her if she wants me to touch her so she can hear me."

"I can see and hear you just fine," Reanna said.

Then Reanna waved a hand in the direction of Cascade.

He blinked and then said to Eve, "Wow you are more beautiful alive than dead."

"Thanks," Eve said, "I think."

At that moment, she realized her dress was still damp, more than likely her nipples were still showing, and she still had her hair wrapped up on top of her head in his car towel. "I got a little wet out there at the crash site."

Then she ignored the feelings of attraction she was getting from Cascade through their touch and looked at Reanna. "If I'm a ghost, how can you see me? And how can Cascade now see me?"

"You are a ghost agent," Reanna said, her voice firm and compact, just as she looked. "You will be recruited to join the Ghost of a Chance Agency and trained by them."

"You lost me with ghost agent thingie," Eve said.

"When a person dies," Reanna said, "almost everyone just goes on into the next life, whatever that is. But for a few thousand around the world, they are asked to stay on as ghost agents and try to help people, as you two did by saving that woman's life this evening."

Eve nodded. "That did feel good."

"I have contacted the head of the Ghost of a Chance agency," Reanna said, "and they will be sending some other agents to help you train and explain everything to you."

Eve nodded, but her disappointment matched what she was feeling from Cascade.

"However," Reanna said, "after your collaboration this afternoon with Officer Cascade, I have also asked if you could be assigned to my department and you and Officer Cascade work together to solve cases."

Reanna turned to Cascade. "Would that would be all right with you?"

"I would be honored," he said.

Eve could feel his excitement at the idea. And she had to

admit that hanging around with Mister Handsome Superhero sounded like a great time to her.

"Would you be interested in such an assignment?" Reanna asked Eve. "You both would be a very special team, the only ghost agent and live superhero working together. It has never been tried. You might work with Poker Boy and his team at times as well as reporting to me. He was very interested in meeting you both once you are up to speed."

She instantly felt Cascade's excitement. It seemed this superhero named Poker Boy and his team often were called on to save the entire world.

So Eve had a chance to go from a worthless husband and a dead job to being someone who could help save people and work with superheroes and gods.

Not counting staying with the hunk of a man sitting across from her. She had no idea how she would figure out the sex problem, but given time, and work, she imagined it might be possible.

How could she say no to that?

"I would be honored," she said out loud.

Reanna smiled and nodded.

Cascade's excitement at her answer sent tingles to places she hadn't felt tingles in a very long time.

Damn, this being dead was going to be a blast.

Who knew?

PART TWO

A Really, Really
Bad Guy

❧◆❧

Eight

EVE BRYSON WAS DEAD.

She knew that for sure now and liked it more than being alive. And now after a month or so, she was getting used to all the perks that came with being dead.

She had avoided anything to do with her funeral and her ex-husband and her old life. She was dead. Even though she was still hanging around the world of the living, she had moved on.

And she had a crush on Deputy McCall Cascade.

More than a crush, actually. She was in lust with him and maybe falling in love with him. Sometimes the two sort of got mixed up.

So even though she had been in Las Vegas training for a month, they had continued to learn about each other as much as they could.

For Eve, the training with two other Ghost of a Chance agents had gone great.

And she had discovered that ghosts had some pretty nifty powers.

For example, she knew how to be inside another person and control that living person. She would never do that with Cascade, but she sure could do it to normal people and who knew when that would come in handy.

And she could teleport anywhere she wanted to go. That allowed her to check in with Cascade during her training every day. They had dinner together every night and both of them loved it.

She got to hear about his day, he got to hear about her training. She loved having someone to talk to.

With the help of a few other superheroes, including the famous Poker Boy and his girlfriend Patty, Eve had her own condo in the Pearl district of Portland.

When Eve had asked how they could do that, Patty had told her that they were so rich they didn't know what to do with all their money, so they could use it as a tax shelter by buying a condo and then not renting it to anyone alive.

Patty and Sherrie, another superhero, even helped Eve furnish her condo the way she wanted it so she had her own place, with dishes, a toilet seat without a lid, and everything.

The other ghost agents found it great that she was working with a superhero as a partner.

A live superhero.

Something very different.

As one of them said, she was doing something that had never been tried before in thousands and thousands of years.

It was going to be interesting to see how it worked out.

Up until a few weeks ago, she didn't even know that any of this ghost and superhero world even existed. But she had to admit, being dead and being a ghost agent was a lot better than being alive and being with the worthless husband she had been stupid enough to marry. She didn't miss him or her old crappy job at all.

Not even for a passing second, which when she thought about it, was very sad. Her living life had been pathetic.

And she really didn't miss being alive in the slightest. This was much, much better.

One of the very weird things about being dead was that the food tasted better. Everything around her seemed more alive as well, and from what one of the other ghost agents had hinted at, the sex was better too.

With other ghost agents.

But she was far, far more interested in having sex with Cascade.

And he seemed to be interested in her as well. He had a smile that could melt the paint off a freeway sign at a half-mile and she loved just sitting across from him over dinner and seeing that smile.

And he said, and she believed him since she could read his thoughts when she wanted, that he loved her long brown hair, her button nose that others found cute and she found sort of weird, and her blue eyes.

She only came up to his chest in height, but since very few people could see them both, that made no difference at all.

The biggest thing was that she could make him laugh and he liked that.

And she loved watching him laugh.

Since she had been inside his head, she knew he liked her, was attracted to her, wanted to be with her. They just hadn't figured out the logistics of a relationship yet between super-hero and ghost. If she had anything to say about it, they would.

Especially the sex part.

It might take time. Both of them had all the time in the world.

She was dead, he was basically immortal.

Worked out perfectly.

Nine

CASCADE HAD REALLY missed Eve during her days away training in Las Vegas. So he had focused on just learning more about the job as deputy sheriff and also more about being a superhero.

He and Reanna had talked a few times. One lunch at a small café with little traffic and decent sandwiches, they had had a great conversation. They had moved out onto an open patio so no one could overhear them. The day wasn't hot yet, but it was warming up quickly. Reanna even took off her hat for the first time since he had known her.

She had longer hair than he had thought she had, but it had been tucked up under her hat and pinned there.

Over a grilled ham and cheese, he had been surprised to find out that he was fairly unique. That only about ten superheroes worked in law enforcement around the United States and less than one hundred total around the world.

"We can't help everyone," Reanna had said as she worked at her club sandwich. "But we try to recruit superheroes like you in critical areas and the Portland area is a critical area into the future."

She didn't explain why and Cascade hadn't pushed.

"I'll have Screamer, who is one of our superheroes and working with Poker Boy at times, come and talk with you. He's a Las Vegas detective."

"Screamer?" Cascade had asked.

"A nickname that has just stuck," Reanna said. "He can read minds and connect two people in thoughts through him. He can also plant images in people's minds and one day got a really nasty slime-ball to give up a location of where he had buried a young girl alive by putting horror images in the guy's mind and making him scream."

"Am I going to be able to do things like that?" Cascade asked, not really sure he liked the idea of making people scream. Not his style.

Reanna had shrugged. "Everyone develops their own powers in their own time. No telling what you will be able to do. Give it time."

The only thing he could do was just nod at that and go back to eating.

After a week of Eve being gone, she appeared in front of him one day while he was eating lunch at Denny's. She was smiling and looking worried at the same time.

"Be right back," she said, looking around and laughing.

Then she vanished again.

Two minutes later she was back, really smiling. "I can teleport anywhere I want!"

He laughed at the excitement in her voice.

"I'm learning a lot," she had said. "You up for dinner tonight?"

"I would love that," he had said. "My place."

And after that, every night for the rest of the month or so of her training, they had had dinner together.

And that made him missing her feel a little less intense.

But when she jumped away every evening to go back to her hotel room in Las Vegas, his apartment once again felt empty.

He had no idea how he could miss a ghost as much as he did.

But there was no doubt how he felt about her.

No doubt in the slightest.

Ten

E VE WAS SO glad that Cascade's boss in the superhero land had given him the power to see and hear her. And so in public all they had to do was be careful that he wasn't seen talking to himself too much, since no one else could see her.

To solve that problem, he had gotten a thin microphone that extended from an earpiece. She had laughed when she saw it and wished she could kiss him for being so smart. Now if someone did see him talking to her, that person would think he was just talking into his microphone.

The only other thing they had to be careful of was the dash camera inside his patrol car when he made stops. That was the only time it came on.

On her first full day back from training with the other ghost agents, she and Cascade had figured it would be a good idea for her to just ride along with him on a standard patrol.

She liked that idea. Neither of them was sure how this "working together" was going to be, so a standard patrol day seemed like a logical place to start.

The first time she had ridden with him in the patrol car to the restaurant, sitting there beside him had felt right to her.

The patrol car smelled faintly of his soap combined with a leather smell from his belt and a computer smell from the equipment between the seats. She liked this car. It had been her refuge from the rain after her car wreck the first hour she was a ghost.

Now she felt comfortable in the front seat beside him, sitting in her jeans and white blouse, her hair pulled back.

He was in his full uniform, blue with dark trim, with a wide-brimmed hat just behind him on the floor between the seats so he could grab it easily.

The Portland July weather was only in the 80s, with bright sun promising to warm up the afternoon.

They had started their patrol at seven in the morning, and since there were no cameras or microphones in the car unless they were stopping someone or in pursuit, they chatted about her training, about the few other ghost agents she had met, and so on.

Then a half-hour into the ride, he saw a speeder in a blue Ford sedan passing cars in a no-passing area.

"There's an accident waiting to happen," she said.

"Let's see if we can stop it from happening," he said, flipping on his lights and pulling out after the speeder.

At that point the inside camera and microphone were

working, so he had to be careful, but she could talk to him out loud just fine, since no one but him could hear her.

As he pulled out after the speeder, Cascade tapped a button on his steering wheel and on the computer screen she could see he was connected to his dispatcher.

Through a shorthand form of talking that she really needed to learn, he gave their location and what he was after and where the speeder was heading.

Eve had never been in a car chasing another car before.

It felt weird.

And exhilarating.

It would have been scary, but nothing could hurt her. So instead she worried about Cascade.

But it was clear he was an expert driver. And very comfortable behind the wheel. Maybe that was one of his superpowers. She would have to ask.

The moment the blue Ford saw Cascade's flashing lights, it signaled and pulled over, sliding to a stop in the gravel shoulder of the highway.

"Guy is in a hurry somewhere," Eve said.

Cascade pulled in behind him, reporting their position.

"Give me a moment to check it out," Eve said.

She knew that cops walking up to a car were in a lot of danger. So she liked how this could be part of her job with him, and help keep him a little safer in a dangerous job.

She went out through the door and up to the driver's side. What she saw through the driver's window shocked her for a moment.

The guy was a young man, sweating, and clearly scared,

his eyes round and his breathing rushed. And slouched down in the passenger seat beside him was a very pregnant wife who was also sweating and shouting in pain. The woman's black hair looked like it was glued to her head.

From the way she was sitting with her legs splayed open and her nightshirt up, she looked to be about to pop a kid right onto the floor mat.

"Shit, just shit!" Eve said and waved for Cascade to hurry.

He got out of the patrol car, walked at a fast pace up beside Eve.

He took one look at the scene and said to the driver. "Can she make it?"

Oh, shit. Eve couldn't help deliver a baby. She was a ghost and wouldn't have a clue what to do anyway.

"I think so," the guy said, glancing at the woman.

"Hurry!" the woman shouted and then screamed in pain.

Eve at that moment was counting her lucky stars she had never been pregnant. That did not look like fun in the slightest.

"Stay on my bumper all the way."

"Thank you, officer," the young, soon-to-be-father said.

Cascade and Eve both ran back to the patrol car and with lights flashing and sirens cutting through the morning air, Cascade pulled out and the blue Ford did the same, staying right with Cascade as he drove and reported in what was happening, alerting the hospital to stand ready.

Six minutes later at the closest hospital, the blue Ford was met with a doctor, a couple nurses, and a stretcher. The almost-mother was rushed inside.

From what Eve could tell, they made it with minutes to spare. That kid really wanted to be born.

Cascade smiled at Eve as they climbed back into the cruiser. "Now that's the kind of thing I wish would happen more often."

"Nice way to start my first day on the job," Eve said, taking a deep breath and relaxing. Just helping a couple get to the hospital had stressed her.

But it was a great way to start the day.

She felt great. And right at that moment she knew she was going to like this job for far more reasons than just being with a hunk of a superhero.

Although, that sure didn't hurt.

Eleven

CASCADE REALLY LIKED the fact that Eve had been able to go up and take a look at the situation in a stopped car. Not only had it saved time today and got a woman in labor to a hospital on time, but Cascade had no doubt her doing that might save his life at some point.

And they had never talked about her doing that. She had just offered to do it automatically.

They were already working as a team and he really liked that more than he wanted to admit.

And that got him thinking about other ways they could work together. He had to get used to the fact that he was the real world side and that she could see and do things he could never see or do.

He could actually arrest someone, but she could read the person's thoughts and find out intent and so much more.

After just one event on their first morning, he now felt even better and actually excited about working with Eve.

The rest of the morning was uneventful and they stopped for lunch at a Denny's Restaurant. Cascade kept his microphone on his head and she sat across from him so they could talk like a normal couple.

He liked that more than he wanted to admit, actually.

He ordered a French Dip and fries, which had sounded good to her as well, so when it came, she just took the ghost component of his meal. Before she took it, they did an experiment. He took a fry and tasted it, then she took the ghost components of everything and he tasted another fry.

The same taste. What she took didn't seem to bother at all what he was eating.

At lunch he told her how he had gone to college, had two degrees, then served four years in the Marines, seeing minor combat in the last stages of the Iraq war. Then he had gone through the police academy and discovered he was really, really good at everything to do with law enforcement.

At one point he asked her why she didn't actually know all of this already since she had been in his mind so much.

"Not surface," she had said. "And I respect your privacy so I never went digging.

And since he could be in her head when she was touching him, he did the same thing. So even though they knew each other's thoughts when touching, they were going to take time, like a regular couple, to learn all the deeper stuff.

And he liked that more than he wanted to admit.

"So is when you joined the force that you were recruited to be a superhero?" Eve asked.

He nodded, finishing off his last fry. "I still don't know much about this superhero business, but I'm learning."

"So we can both learn together," she said, laughing.

"I like that idea a lot," he said.

And he did.

Twelve

EVE REALLY HAD enjoyed their lunch. She wanted to learn everything about Cascade without digging into his mind, even though she now knew how to do that easily. But for the time, with him, she would stay on the surface, and she knew he was doing the same with her when inside her head.

That showed that not only did they both care for each other, they both respected each other.

She couldn't remember if she had ever had a boyfriend who respected her in any fashion at all.

After lunch, they headed back out on patrol and thirty minutes later were working along a winding two-lane paved road that stayed next to a river and connected two of the smaller towns outside of Portland.

It seemed that Deputy Sheriff Cascade's territory to patrol was very, very large. The county was underfunded and thus the sheriff's department understaffed. Every day on patrol they were going to cover a lot of territory, much of it Eve had never seen before.

As they came around a corner, Eve spotting an old white panel van tucked up in the pine trees on her side. Something about it gave her a chill and she mentioned that to Cascade.

"Let's take a look," he said, frowning. "One thing I have been learning to trust is that gut-sense about things. Seems to come from somewhere."

He reported in where they were, what he was investigating, and then pulled up the small dirt road off the pavement and parked a distance behind the van.

The van was in a small clearing where the road turned around. Sun beat down on the panel van, but the trees around it looked dark and very uninviting.

Cascade started to run the plates while Eve got out to see what was happening.

As she did, a man came back down a trail out of the trees with a shovel. He had on bib overalls, a dirty white T-shirt under them, and heavy boots. He looked muddy, like he had been digging a while.

She had no idea really where they were at, but she had a hunch digging anything in this area was going to be illegal unless this guy owned the land, and from the looks of him, his greasy black hair and an old panel van, that seemed unlikely.

And as she saw him, every alarm bell she had in her head went off. Something was very wrong with him and it took her a moment to see it.

When in training the last few weeks, she had learned to look at people's auras. Her aura was extremely bright and full of colors, but she had it contained behind a shield because she was a ghost and even ghosts had enemies, she was told.

Cascade had a very, very bright aura as well, and her aura and his seemed to match in a lot of places. That had pleased her more than she wanted to admit, but so far had never told Cascade.

She had also learned that human auras often told a good story about who the person was.

This man's aura was black and very small.

He saw the sheriff's car and she could see him hesitate, clearly trying to calm himself and keep walking toward his van as if nothing was wrong.

"Time to see what you have been up to," Eve said.

She moved toward him and just let him walk right through her.

Evil.

Pure evil.

No wonder his aura was pure black. He didn't have a redeeming feature about him.

The guy had just buried a young girl he had killed, had another at his home in a basement, and was thinking about how he was now going to have to bury a cop as well. It didn't worry him, just annoyed him.

He had no guilt, no sense of anything but that he owned the world and could do what he pleased with other people's lives.

Eve let the man walk on, then she just bent over and threw up her lunch.

Never, in all her life, had she experienced anything like that. She had no idea that people like this man even existed on the planet.

As she tried to gather herself from the horrid thoughts of that piece of trash, behind her she heard Cascade open his car door and climb out.

Shit!

She had to do something. This guy had a large pistol stuck in his belt and was about to just gun down Cascade without a hesitation.

And Cascade was too far away to warn in any real way.

She turned and in three steps was back inside the blackness that was the guy she called human trash.

He had his hand on the revolver and was turned slightly toward his van to set down the shovel. He planned to set the shovel down, draw the revolver and kill Cascade.

But not on her watch.

Not on her first day.

Not today.

Not any damn day, actually.

She made him freeze like something had encased him in metal.

She could feel his panic start to rise as he tried to move.

"Nope, trash man. No moving for you."

The guy panicked even more hearing her voice.

Cascade must have seen her throw up, then turn and go back inside the guy. Cascade hadn't moved more than a step from his patrol car and he had his hand on his service pistol, but hadn't drawn it yet.

If she hadn't stopped this trash, Cascade would have never gotten that gun out in time to defend himself.

"Step away from the van!" Cascade shouted at the man.

The dashboard camera on the patrol car was operating, feeding a live stream back to headquarters, so she and Cascade were going to have to be careful how they handled this.

Eve decided she had had enough of the disgust in this guy's mind and with a simple tweak of a nerve that she had learned how to do in the last two weeks, she put the guy to sleep.

He fell to the ground and, as he did, his hand came out holding the large gun.

Eve stepped aside, trying to use the fresh afternoon air to clear her head. They had to save that girl at the guy's house. The girl was young and was in a metal box in his cellar. The trash had doubted she would be alive when he got back, since he planned on stopping for lunch along the way.

But the trash didn't care if the girl lived or died. He actually enjoyed playing with a dead girl's body at least until they started to smell and stiffen up.

That thought almost made Eve throw up again.

She glanced back at the piece of smelly trash slumped on the ground. He would be out for about ten minutes.

Cascade instantly had his gun out and was approaching the guy as he had been trained, calling for backup as he did.

"He buried a girl up in the trees beside a couple others he killed over the last year," Eve said.

Cascade nodded slightly, looking stunned.

"We got another girl in an airtight box in his basement," Eve said. "She isn't going to last much longer."

"Shit," Cascade said, softly.

Cascade got near the guy, kicked the guy over, shoved the gun aside, and then managed to get handcuffs on the guy.

Eve moved over to Cascade and touched him so they could talk inside his head.

"I can go into that trash again, wake him, get him to confess," she said.

"You can do that?" Cascade asked without speaking.

"Never done it, but been trained how and watched it a couple times," she said, showing Cascade her training. "If I get the trash to repent and tell us about the girl locked in his basement, we have a reason to get officers there quickly."

"Where is the trash's house?" Cascade asked without saying a word.

"Down off of I-5," she said. "Too far for us to make it in time to save her."

"Do it," Cascade said.

She let go of him and moved back to the piece of human garbage on the ground. Then she stepped into him again.

The blackness was intense, more than she had ever imagined it could be.

She got him to wake up and Cascade ordered the man to stay on his knees facing the patrol car and its camera.

Eve got the trash to do as Cascade ordered. Then she

made the trash start bawling and sobbing like one of the girls he had killed.

"I don't want to do this anymore," the trash sobbed.

Then Eve, through the sobs, and loud enough for Cascade's microphone to pick up, got the trash to tell all about the women buried up the hill and how he wanted to save the girl in his basement.

Eve got the trash to tell Cascade his address and where the girl was exactly.

Then Eve had the guy say, "Hurry. I don't want another death on my conscience."

Eve knew this piece of human trash didn't have a conscience, but what the hell, it sounded good.

At that moment a second patrol car arrived, lights flashing, and another officer about Cascade's size and build, only with blond hair, scrambled up beside Cascade.

Eve got the trash to repeat what he had just said.

Cascade called it in, getting officers and medical personnel rushing to the man's house.

Eve decided that this man needed even more punishment.

Jewel, one of the other ghost agents who had been a doctor before she died, had shown her how to change a person's brain in a way that caused the person extreme pain at times.

Eve had never thought she would use that, so hadn't paid a lot of attention. But she wanted more than anything to use it now. So she needed help. This guy deserved that kind of punishment.

She tweaked the nerve again and the guy pitched forward flat onto his face in the dirt.

Eve stepped out and shouted into the air, "Jewel, need some help!"

Jewel had said to just call into the air when she needed help. And if Jewel could do what she said was possible, this was going to be fun.

Thirteen

CASCADE KNEW WITHOUT reading Eve's thoughts that she had just saved his life.

That guy would have had that big gun up and firing before Cascade had a chance to even draw or duck for cover.

And the idea that he had come that close to death made him shake a little.

He had known something was wrong when Eve had left the guy and thrown up. He should have reacted differently right then. But that would come with more time together.

This was still only their first day. They needed to learn a lot more about each other.

Then when Eve had shown him what was in the guy's head and what he had done and about the girl in the basement about to die, Cascade had wanted to throw up as well.

Then Eve did something he couldn't imagine doing. She

offered to go back inside an evil man's head and make him confess to try to save the girl.

Eve was a lot, lot stronger than even she thought she was. Wow.

She got the guy to wake up and get on his knees, facing the camera on the patrol car and speaking loud enough to be picked up by Cascade's microphone. Then the guy confessed twice, once to Cascade and a second time as Jimmy, another sheriff's deputy, arrived on scene.

Cascade got emergency police headed to the guy's home with an ambulance.

Then, as he was finished, Eve put the guy to sleep again and stepped out of the evil.

Then she did something that Cascade hadn't expected.

She called for another ghost agent. The one that had trained Eve over the last month or so.

Was something more happening?

What was wrong?

A woman appeared who seemed to be about Eve's age. The woman, who Cascade assumed was Jewel because that was who Eve had called for, was wearing a thin tan bikini under an open shimmering robe. And she could wear that bikini.

Her hair was pulled back and she had suntan lotion on that smelled slightly of coconut butter.

The woman nodded at Cascade who kept a pose as if he couldn't see a woman in a skimpy bikini standing near a murderer in the pine trees in Oregon.

"Looks like the problem is pretty well covered here," Jewel

said, taking a glance at the man on the ground. She turned to Eve. "So why the call?"

"Piece of trash there killed a bunch of women," Eve said, "just buried one up in the trees here, and has another he planned to play with when he got home, dead or alive, locked in a metal box in his basement."

"Shit," Jewel said, shaking her head and then looking with disgust at the man sprawled on the ground.

Then she smiled and turned back to Eve. "Now I understand. You think this guy deserves a little more punishment than this fine, handsome policeman can give him?"

"I do," Eve said, winking at Cascade. "And I know you showed me how, but damned if I trust myself enough on my first day to try it."

"Come with me," Jewel said, taking Eve's hand.

And as Cascade watched, his ghost partner and a woman in a bikini vanished inside the body of an evil killer.

Just vanished.

Fourteen

E VE DIDN'T WANT to go back inside the piece of trash, but with Jewel with her, it felt better.

Hand-in-hand, they both went into the evil blackness that was the piece of trash's mind.

"Oh, one of the worst I have seen," Jewel said to Eve.

Eve could feel Jewel actually shudder.

"I hope to not see another this bad in a lot of years," Eve said.

"They are out there, sadly," Jewel said. "That's why we have the jobs we do."

Then, in the back of the man's brain, Jewel once again took Eve step-by-step through the process of how to make certain thoughts generate extreme pain.

It seems that Jewel had been a medical doctor before being killed and becoming a ghost agent. And that medical training came in handy a lot.

Together, Eve and Jewel set the thoughts that would cause this trash pile of a human being pain. Since he hadn't cared about the pain of his victims, it seemed like a fair justice to have him now feel some of that pain.

They left the trash, still hand-in-hand, laughing.

Cascade watched them appear, one eyebrow up in question.

Two other cop cars had just arrived.

"We just gave this trash something to think about is all," Eve said to Cascade.

"I think you'll find it amusing," Jewel said to Cascade. "And nice meeting you. Take care of our new recruit."

He nodded and Jewel vanished.

At that moment, the piece of trash on the ground started to moan and try to struggle back to his knees.

The third cop coming up to the group said, "Great job, Cascade. They got the girl out of the box in this guy's basement and she's alive and on her way to the hospital."

Eve applauded and Cascade smiled.

"Read him his rights," Eve said, "And I'll get him to confess again."

Cascade put his gun away, got out the rights card in his shirt pocket and started reading the trash his rights as if he was a real human being.

Eve went back inside the dark, evil brain one more time and got the guy to cry slightly again.

"Do you understand your rights?" Cascade asked the trash.

"I do," she got the guy to say.

That was on the dash camera and an officer cam one of the other officers was wearing.

"Would you like to tell us what you were doing up that hill there?" Cascade asked.

She got the trash, through tears and sobs to make it believable, explain how he buried another body up there and where everyone he had killed was buried. And then she got him to confess to kidnapping and putting the girl in the box in his basement with the intent of killing her and having sex with her dead body.

"You are one sick piece of trash," the blond cop said as Eve left the guy.

The two new cops on the scene moved to pull the guy up from his knees.

"Ask him if he enjoyed making love to the girls," Eve said to Cascade, smiling.

Cascade did and the piece of trash started to smile. Then the trash got this horrid look and screamed in agony and went to the ground, peeing himself as he did.

"Oh, great," one of the cops said.

The two cops yanked him back to his feet and started to drag him toward their cars.

The trash just kept screaming.

Eve went over to Cascade and put her hand on his shoulder.

"What did you and that other ghost Jewel do to the human trash?" Cascade asked without saying anything out loud.

"We just rewired his brain a slight bit is all," Eve said,

laughing. "Now when he thinks about sex with anyone, boy or girl, young or old, it will feel like someone has kicked him in the groin really hard."

"You didn't?" he thought at her, but she could tell it was everything he could do to not burst out laughing.

"Other ghosts have done this to perverts and killers like this one," Eve told him. "So many times in fact, the problem is starting to get known in the medical community."

"I think I love this job," Cascade said.

"As soon as those guy's memories fade from my mind," Eve said, "I will as well."

Fifteen

"MEMORIES ALMOST FADED?" Cascade asked her as the two of them sat in his living room, facing each other, sipping on a wonderful white wine. He had cooked them both a fantastic dinner of stuffed sage hen and steamed vegetables. Best meal she remembered tasting in a long time.

She said she felt bad that she couldn't cook for him but he could cook for her, since she could eat the ghost part of his meal. That was when she discovered that he loved to cook, had thought of being a chef instead of a cop after the Marines. So the fact that he could cook something for himself and have two people enjoy it was wonderful to him.

This handsome superhero really was too good to be true.

"Memories from the trash are gone," she said, smiling at him. "One of the nice things about being a ghost, the memories of people we brush through or are inside of don't stick with us for very long."

He raised his glass. "To a good first day, partner. Thanks for saving my life."

"I think that's what partners are for," she said.

After that they watched a movie and both of them fell asleep on the couch together, her inside him.

It felt wonderful to sleep with him like that.

Natural.

He woke up first and stirred her and she agreed she would see him bright and early in the morning for their second day.

He wanted her to stay and she wanted to stay. But they would have time to talk about that soon enough.

Days of time riding around in a patrol car, actually.

She jumped to her condo, which actually felt empty.

She should be staying with him, making love to him.

Or at least sleeping in his arms as they had done on the couch.

She was a ghost, he was a superhero. Somehow, someone, somewhere, would know what she and Cascade could do to take the relationship to the next level.

They both wanted to.

She took a quick shower, then crawled into her wonderful bed, thinking about him.

He was handsome and he could cook and he liked her.

And today they had saved a life and helped a child be born safely.

Pretty damn fine first day together.

She fell asleep thinking of his wonderful smile.

And she was pretty sure she had a smile on her face as well.

PART THREE

Saving More Lives

Sixteen

HOW CAN A ghost make love to a live superhero? That was the problem that Eve and Cascade had been trying to figure out for their first full month as a team. So far, without success.

But even with that minor problem, the first month had been fantastic as far as Cascade was concerned.

They shared everything else.

So everyday he was on duty, Eve rode with him. And she saw things that at times he missed. She could see a person's aura and from what he had seen through her thoughts, a bad person's aura was mostly black.

So not only did they go looking for speeders and do their standard patrols, but they also went looking for black auras.

And in their first month they had found a couple.

The first had been on their first day with the killer, but the second major black aura on a person had been during their third week together.

They had just finished with lunch at a nice dinner called Mary's beside the large mall near Tigard, Oregon. They were walking back toward the patrol car when Eve touched his arm and had him stop.

He could sense she was alarmed.

"Look through my eyes," she said.

They had practiced that a few times and it always felt weird.

He turned with her and mostly closed his own eyes because otherwise he would be seeing through his own eyes and hers and that had made him dizzy almost every time.

What she was seeing was a man in jeans, a long duster-like coat buttoned up even though it was almost ninety degrees, and tennis shoes. He had a shaved head and sunglasses covering his eyes.

"Look at his aura," Eve said.

"Black," he said.

"Sickly black," Eve said as Cascade opened his own eyes and looked at the man walking along the edge of the mall toward an entrance.

Every alarm in his head was going off.

"Jewel told me when someone had a sickly black aura, they were about to commit something truly evil."

"Let's go!" Cascade said.

He was carrying a portable mike and reported in at once where he was at, what he had seen, and that he needed backup at once.

"I'm going to see if I can catch him and find out what's going on," Eve said.

At a run, she headed for him just as he reached the mall entrance.

It was then, with Eve still a good fifty yards from the man, that the guy opened up his trench coat and pulled out what looked to be some form of automatic rifle. It was nothing like a gun that Cascade had seen before.

Clearly something Russian or Chinese and it had a very large magazine inserted in it.

That gun was made for killing.

On a run toward the man, Cascade called in an update and then had his gun out.

At that point a few people started screaming and running away from the man.

Eve went right through a couple of the people and then saw the man had the gun out and was lifting it.

She instantly jumped to beside him.

And then vanished inside the guy.

The guy froze and dropped the gun.

Eve had just saved a lot of lives.

Seventeen

❧

EVE HATED BEING inside of sick humans.

And this guy named Calvin was as sick as they came. He just wanted to kill people and had actually been looking forward to killing a lot of people in the mall and then some police.

Calvin was young, not more than twenty. A high-school dropout and a person his parents and family had disowned.

Calvin was going to show them he could amount to something.

He knew if he did a lot of killing, the press would make him famous because that's what they did. If you killed enough people, you got famous.

And he wanted to be famous.

He wanted his parents to know he was famous.

He knew that people should worship him and follow him

and he needed the press and everyone to know he could carry through and earn their respect by killing.

Eve was disgusted at the very belief.

She froze him down solid and got him to drop his gun.

Then she was about to tweak his nerve to put him asleep when she realized he had a friend.

A friend as sick as he was.

Lewis.

Same age.

Same sickness.

Lewis wanted to be famous as well.

Their plan was for Calvin to go into the mall first, start killing people, get the people stampeding toward the other side of the mall and Lewis would kill them as they ran toward him.

Eve snapped the nerve on Calvin and he dropped the floor, out like a light just as Cascade reached them.

"He's got a friend on the other side of the mall," Eve said. "Get help there quick. I'll see if I can stop him in time."

Cascade nodded and was calling in instructions again.

Eve instantly jumped to the other side of the mall.

Lewis also had on a long coat and still had it buttoned. And he was looking puzzled because people were moving toward him, but there had been no shots fired.

Eve merged inside of him.

This kid was as sick as his friend. And was excited about killing and becoming famous.

"Not today, asshole," Eve said to the sick brain.

She had the kid open his coat and then put his hands over

his head. Then she had him lean back against the wall so the police that had just pulled up outside would see him.

Then she had an idea.

A nasty idea, but an idea.

She went back to the part of the kid's brain where Jewel had shown her with the girl killer a few weeks back. And there she set a command and rewired his brain just a little bit.

At that point the police got there.

Five of them approached and got the kid's gun and got him on the ground.

Then she left him, standing off to one side to watch.

He wanted to be famous. Well, he was going to be famous for crying his eyes out anytime his name was mentioned.

For the moment, the kid looked defiant and smiling. People were taking pictures of him on their cell phones.

"What's your name?" one of the cops asked.

The kid started to say Lewis and burst into tears and collapsed on the ground.

Eve looked around at all the people filming the gunman crying like a baby and laughed.

She jumped back to Cascade. He and three other cops had the unconscious Calvin handcuffed and on his stomach on the ground.

She touched Cascade's arm. "Got the other one."

"Great," Cascade said in his inner voice. "Are we done?"

"Don't know," Eve said. She had a feeling she had missed something.

So she said, "I'm going back into this guy to see if there's anything we missed."

"Good idea," Cascade said, again in his inner voice.

Eve crawled inside the guy and got him to wake up some.

He had no idea why his plan hadn't worked. But then she saw that he had a second plan.

And his second plan would kill even more than he would have killed here in the mall today.

They had two cars loaded with explosives from his grandfather's factory. He had driven one and Lewis had driven the other.

The bombs would level both sides of the mall and both parking lots on the sides of the mall away from where he and Lewis had entered.

And they were set to go off in exactly twenty-six minutes. Just as the police were emptying the mall.

Eve quickly rewired this idiot's brain as well to make him proclaim his plan over and over and over anytime anyone asked him any kind of question. And to proclaim his superiority over everyone else as well.

And she also had him tell anyone who was listening how to defuse the bombs he had built.

And he would do that over and over for the rest of his life.

He was not going to be popular in prison.

And he would deserve everything he got there, if he lived to get that far.

Eighteen

CASCADE WATCHED AS Eve appeared out of the gunman and moved over beside him.

Two cops had the gunman pinned and were about to bring him to his feet.

"Both of their cars are rigged with massive amounts of explosives to go off in just over twenty minutes."

"Shit," Cascade said in his inner voice.

"Their cars are parked at the other two main entrances," Eve said, touching Cascade and showing him what she knew about defusing the bombs.

Cascade nodded.

"Ask him to tell you how to defuse the bombs," Eve said.

Cascade nodded and stepped toward Calvin.

"Any more of you idiots beside you and your partner on the other side of the mall?" Cascade demanded. "Anything else like bombs in your cars?"

Calvin smiled and then got a frown as he started telling Cascade all about the bombs and his great plan to kill even more people."

Cascade felt disgusted. He could only imagine how Eve felt crawling around inside the guy's head.

"How do we disarm them?" Cascade demanded.

Calvin was frowning, but he rattled off how exactly to disarm them, how to go in the passenger door and the detonator was on the floor of the passenger seat.

There were now five cops there.

Cascade asked what both cars looked like and Calvin told them, proclaiming how smart he was and how many people were going to die.

"Can we trust him?" Officer Daniels of the Tigard Department asked.

Cascade knew him as a good guy and really smart and a cop who often ran in when calling for help might have been a better solution.

"I think we can," Cascade said, nodding. "Get the bomb squad on the way and close off those entrances and get people leaving the mall through this and the entrance with the other gunman. I'll take the car on the west side."

Daniels nodded. "I'll take the east side."

At that Cascade turned and went around the mall toward the west at full run while Daniels went the other way.

As he came around the corner he saw Eve pointing at the car he needed to find.

He shouted for a couple of people near other cars to run and they did.

"Sure wish I could teleport like you do," he said to Eve as he got to the car winded.

"More than likely you can," Eve said. "Other superheroes can. You just haven't learned how yet. So if this bomb starts to go, you just think you want to be back by the patrol car real hard."

"Is that possible?" he asked as he stared in at the massive explosives filling the back seat of the car.

"Believe it is," Eve said. "I have no intention of losing a partner this soon in our relationship.

He nodded.

With that, he took a deep breath and opened the passenger door.

And nothing exploded.

So far, so good.

Nineteen

E ve watched as Cascade followed the guy's instructions perfectly, leaning over the passenger seat and working with the detonator on the floor.

Within one minute he had the bomb defused.

He stood and stepped back.

She touched him.

On the outside he seemed cool and collected, but he was waves of relief inside.

She said to him that she wished she could kiss him for that great work.

"Thanks," he said. "Think you can help Daniels?"

"I can if you move away from this car," she said.

"Gladly," he said, moving back and waving even more people out of the area.

She jumped to the other side of the mall.

Daniels had the passenger door of the other car open, but

seemed to be having issues with something. He was just staring at the detonator.

She merged with him.

As Cascade had thought, Daniels was a good guy, living with a life partner who worked for Intel. They were considering trying to adopt.

And he loved being a cop. He loved helping people.

But he was having trouble remembering exactly which way to go. He had started to doubt himself and was about to back out and let the car explode.

She carefully fed him some confidence and the correct instructions in such a way that he wouldn't realize he got it from anything but himself.

He nodded, took a deep breath and went back to work on the bomb.

Eve stayed with him, keeping him completely focused and sure of the instructions.

And with eight minutes to spare, he had the bomb disarmed.

Then she planted the thought, "Just to be sure, back the hell out of here and clear the area."

He did just that and as he left the car, she turned and left him.

He did exactly what Cascade was doing on the other side of the mall. He waved people away, then headed for the mall doors to get people away from the big glass doors and back down the hallway.

If that thing blew after all, it wouldn't kill anyone, but it was going to make an awful mess.

She jumped back to Cascade and smiled at him. "He's got it."

Cascade smiled, then said to everyone in the mall close to the doors. "Everyone down or take cover," he said. "Just in case."

Nothing exploded.

As far as Eve was concerned, tonight they were having a great dinner and wine and she just might do whatever she could to have sex with the handsome man who had saved a lot of lives today.

Of course, it didn't work. He was a human and she was a ghost.

But it was still a wonderful dinner.

PART FOUR

They Don't Want to Sleep

Twenty

FOR A GHOST and a superhero, what exactly was the next level?

He could see her just fine, but they couldn't really touch each other. Granted, being in each other's minds was pretty damn nifty as far as she was concerned, but they were both very, very horny.

So far they had managed to avoid it because they had no answer to how to have a physical relationship. But Eve knew they had to solve this very, very frustrating problem.

And fast.

So on Saturday afternoon, Eve decided to go try to get some answers.

Cascade was stretched out in front of the television by 9 in the morning in his apartment, and she had no doubt he would be asleep in ten minutes. Having a ghost in his head all the time was tiring. He hadn't been a superhero much longer than she had been a ghost, so all this was new for both of them.

She was tired as well.

But the sex thing needed to get solved.

She had set up a meeting with Jewel and her boyfriend, Tommy, at their normal breakfast place, the Golden Nugget Buffet in Las Vegas. So with an air kiss to her partner, she jumped from outside Portland, Oregon, to Vegas.

Tommy had been a cop when alive and Jewel a doctor. They were the two Ghost of a Chance agents that had trained her in what she could do as an agent in this new life, and she had called Jewel a couple of times the first month for different forms of help.

This morning, Jewel had on a beautiful blue blouse and had her long brown hair pulled back off her face. Tommy had on a T-shirt with a light shirt over it. With his close-cut brown hair, he reminded Eve a lot of Cascade.

Both Jewel and Tommy were tall and exercised every day a great deal, mostly running.

Jewel and Tommy had both died in a car wreck as she had done. They had just met and as a deputy, he was driving Jewel, as a doctor, to an emergency in the Montana mountains when a deer jumped in front of them and they had hit a tree.

As had happened to Eve, instead of crossing over, Jewel had remained in this real world and been recruited as a Ghost of a Chance agent. Jewel and Tommy had been recruited as agents together and had fallen in love.

Eve liked Jewel and Tommy a great deal and felt as if she could trust them with anything.

They had already finished their breakfast and were sipping on coffee when she arrived.

In one month, eating had become one of her real pleasures in being dead, besides being with Cascade. And being able to read other people's thoughts and walk though things. That was all fun as well, but mostly she just loved every minute with Cascade.

Jewel and Tommy were much later morning people than she and Cascade were, because of his job schedule. Jewel and Tommy had just finished breakfast, for her it was getting closer to lunch.

The Golden Nugget had a wonderful feel about it. Brown cloth decorations, brown oak wood, and large windows looking out over the pool gave the place a feeling of relaxation instead of Las Vegas hurry-up-and-spend of so many of the casinos.

There were only about twenty live humans scattered around the large room and Jewel and Tommy had a table off to one side near a planter. It seemed that they always had that table. Live humans never sat there.

When Eve had trained here in Vegas after her death, she and Jewel and Tommy had spent a lot of time right here in this buffet at the same table.

The smell of bacon and waffles filled the air and even though she had eaten a few hours before, she went for a waffle as dessert. Damn she was loving to eat, but Jewel had warned

Eve that she had better get exercising fairly quickly. It seemed that ghosts could gain weight, and with as good as food tasted, Eve could see how it wouldn't be hard to stack on the pounds.

Eve joined Jewel and Tommy and they asked about her and Cascade's first month and she filled them in as she worked on her waffle.

"I sometimes miss just riding on patrol," Tommy said. "It was always a combination of quiet boredom combined at times with acute awareness and broken by moments of panicked action."

"Would you leave this life for that again?" Jewel asked him.

He laughed. "Not a chance."

All three of them laughed, then Jewel focused on Eve. "So what's the problem?"

Eve took a deep breath, trying to figure out where to start. Then she decided to just tell them what was happening instead of asking questions around the problem.

"Cascade and I have fallen in love," she said.

"Wow, that's wonderful to hear," Jewel said, smiling a huge grin.

"It will sure make spending all those hours together a lot more fun," Tommy said, also smiling.

"It is fun," Eve said. "More than either of us have ever experienced before. We are sharing things I didn't know I would ever share with anyone else. And he's just an amazingly special person."

"So what's the problem?" Jewel asked.

Tommy laughed and looked at his partner, shaking his head at Jewel. "Sex."

"Oh," Jewel said, suddenly sitting back as she realized Eve's problem.

"Yeah," Eve said. "The problem, put bluntly, is that Cascade and I are beyond horny and damned if we can figure out the ghost-and-alive-connection problem."

"Oh," Jewel said again.

Eve pushed the remains of her waffle away. From Jewel's reaction, this was not going to be an easy problem to solve.

If there was a solution at all.

Twenty-One

"WE NEED SOME help with this one," Jewel said.

Tommy nodded.

And before Eve could stop Jewel or even ask who the help might be, Jewel said into the air, "K.J., a little help."

"Need a minute to finishing getting dressed if you don't mind." A voice in the air above the table seemed to echo from a deep chamber.

Eve looked around, but, of course, no one was there.

Jewel turned to Eve. "K.J. is our team's boss. He is the one who reports to the gods and he is the one who gets us our assignments, unlike you and Cascade who just go out and save people."

"Good thinking," Tommy said to Jewel. "K.J. has been dead for over a hundred years and has a reputation as a party person."

"One of the best, if not the best party person," a man said, appearing next to the table. "Please, if you must spread my reputation, do it with some accuracy."

The guy was short, really, really short, wearing a gray pinstriped silk suit and vest, a pink tie with flamingos on it, pink slippers, and a bright pink feathery hat that had a tail on it that went down his back.

Eve just stared, her mouth open. Her life in Oregon had been sheltered, clearly.

He bowed slightly to Eve, the feathers in his hat flowing around him. "I am K.J. I have heard you are a fast study."

"I had good instructors," Eve managed to say, nodding to Tommy and Jewel.

K.J. glanced at the buffet, then looked at Jewel. "Before I move to get some maple syrup on this grand tie, what is your problem?"

Jewel indicated that K.J. should sit down at the table.

"A major issue I see," K.J. said, sitting.

"You have heard," Jewel said, "that Eve is the first ghost agent to partner with a live superhero."

"How is that going?" K.J. said. "A grand experiment, if I must say."

"We are doing well," Eve said. "Saved a bunch of lives so far."

"And that is why we are here in this ghostly state," K.J. said, nodding.

"But Eve and her partner, Deputy McCall Cascade, have a problem," Jewel said.

"You are with Cascade?" K.J. said, his eyes lighting up.

Eve was surprised, because in all the times inside of Cascade's head, she had never seen a thought about this sparklingly-dressed ghost. She was sure she would have remembered. And positive Cascade would have remembered K.J. as well.

"I am," she said.

"Oh, girl, how do you keep your hands off of that hunk of a man?" K.J. asked. "I saw his picture when he was recruited and got so hot I had to retire for the day and take care of issues."

Eve was fairly certain her face was bright red.

Jewel and Tommy were both laughing.

"That's the problem we called you here about," Jewel finally said.

"I can see no problem at all with climbing all over that hunk of a man," K.J. said. He looked at Eve. "Is it dreamy to be riding with him in his masculine patrol car with all the leather seats and the wonderful tools of manhood?"

She blushed again and laughed. "It is dreamy, yes."

"I knew it would be," K.J. said, clapping his hands. "Just knew it. You are one lucky ghost, girl."

"I think so," Eve said.

"So," Jewel said, between laughter. "How do they go about having sex?"

K.J. looked at Jewel, then back to Eve with a sly grin on his face.

"Oh, girl you are a fast mover, aren't you?"

Twenty-Two

E VE FIGURED HER face was about as red as it was going to get, so she smiled at K.J. Then said, "Do you blame me?"

"Oh, my, not at all," K.J. said, fanning himself.

Eve thought Tommy was going to fall out of his chair laughing.

Jewel was trying to hold it together enough to actually get an answer out of K.J.

Eve was really starting to like this crazy ghost of a boss.

"So, what is needed," Jewel asked, "for these two to have sex? Real sex."

"Passion," K.J. said, "but with that hunk of a man, I doubt that is your problem, is it?"

"It is not," Eve said, smiling at him. "And it is not his problem toward me either. We both want this, but both of us are so new to our worlds, we have no idea how to go about that part of a relationship."

"Like two teenagers in the backseat of a car," K.J. said. "The fumbling is half the fun I am told."

"All I remember is the fear and the worry and the sweating," Jewel said.

Again, Tommy just laughed and shook his head.

Eve hadn't had any experience in back seats of cars. And her first sexual experiences hadn't been that rewarding, actually. And her sexual experiences with her loser of a husband hadn't changed that. So with Cascade, she was hoping for a little more.

Actually, a lot more.

K.J. looked at her. "You ever read the fine short story 'Man of Steel, Woman of Kleenex'?"

Eve shook her head. She had no idea what he was talking about.

Again Tommy laughed and Jewel just looked at K.J. with a stern look.

"No?" K.J. asked Eve. "For the better, since even though Cascade is a superhero and someone can put a hand through you like Kleenex, the situation in the story does not apply."

Tommy had to catch himself from laughing himself off his chair. If they hadn't been ghosts, everyone in the place would have been staring at them.

"K.J.," Jewel said, pretending to put on a stern face. "This is a serious problem that these two young lovers are trying to solve."

K.J. was laughing with Tommy at his own joke, but finally nodded and took a moment to catch his breath.

Eve was going to have to look up that story just to see why they were laughing.

Finally K.J. looked at both Jewel and Tommy. "I will teach you all a very nifty trick that none of your team knows yet, but that might come in handy at times."

He glanced around, clearly to make sure none of the live customers were watching, even though none of the four of them could be seen. Then K.J. reached forward and picked up the Keno ticket holder in the center of the table.

Not just the ghost element of the ticket holder, but the entire holder.

Then he set it down on the table with an audible click, smiling.

"Damn," Tommy said. "How did you do that?"

K.J. pointed to his head. "Just as we do all of our skills. I just imagined it."

"So we can cross over into the real world without controlling a person to do it for us?" Jewel asked, clearly as stunned as Eve was feeling.

"Within limits," K.J. said. "As far as I know, a normal human can't see us no matter what we do. Something about light and things I didn't understand."

"Cascade can see me fine thanks to Reanna," Eve said.

"Makes sense because he's a superhero," K.J. said, nodding.

K.J. then stood and indicated all three of them should follow him over to a planter filled with artificial plants that divided the buffet from a small lobby at the top of an escalator.

"Put your hand through the plants," K.J. said to each of them.

They all did.

Eve had gotten used to walking through things and not feeling a thing. She actually kind of liked it.

"Now," K.J. said, "Imagine your hand is solid enough to move a plant leaf."

Eve used what Jewel and Tommy had taught her about imagining being in different places and just being there, and floating, and so on. All of her training had been on using her imagination. It seemed that ghosts felt like they were part of this world, but were not really, so then had what seemed like powers to jump anywhere they could imagine or float places, or make others do as a ghost wanted.

Ghosts felt like they were tied to this world, but actually were not, thus their imagination had to break them free.

Eve focused that same imagination energy on making her hand solid and touching the plant leaf.

And suddenly she could feel the leaf. Not the ghost element of the leaf, that had a certain feel, but the actual artificial leaf.

It moved under her touch.

Jewel and Tommy had the same success.

"Wonderful! K.J. said, clapping his hands like a teenager happy to see someone.

He turned and went back to the table. As he did, Eve watched him study the room to make sure no one was looking, then he pulled out a chair that was tucked in too close to the table.

Not the ghost part of the chair, but the actual chair.

To any live person watching, either in the restaurant or on a camera, that chair must have looked like it had moved by itself.

Jewel, Tommy, and Eve tried to move a chair, but even though they all could feel the chair's surface, they couldn't get enough grip or energy to move it.

"This takes time and practice to learn," K.J. said as they all sat back down.

Then he turned to Eve. "But I have discovered over the years, after many pleasurable nights in my oversized hot tub with wonderful and very-much-alive superheroes who could see me, the practice is very much worth the effort."

Eve was again convinced she was blushing.

"That's how you and Madge from the diner did it," Tommy said, smiling.

Eve figured he was clearly talking about an event before she had died. She would ask later.

"A fella doesn't kiss and tell," K.J. said, laughing.

Jewel just laughed and shook her head.

"If I can make my hand solid to touch something," Eve asked, "can I make other parts of my body solid as well for Cascade's touch?"

K.J. smiled and fanned himself again with an imaginary fan. "With practice, Mr. Hunk Cascade can feel any part of you that you would want him to feel."

Eve was about to jump up and down for joy.

She smiled at Jewel and Tommy. "Thank you both."

Then she stood and moved over and kissed K.J. solidly on the cheek.

"And thank you," Eve said to K.J. "And now I need to go do some practicing on Cascade's wonderful and very masculine body."

"I think I might have the vapors just thinking of that," K.J. said, again fanning himself.

She laughed and jumped back to Cascade's apartment.

He was stretched out on the couch, sound asleep. She knelt by the couch and then gently touched his face.

The light stubble on his cheeks felt wonderful against her hand.

He stirred as she brushed his cheek again. He smiled and opened his eyes.

"That felt wonderful," he said, looking into her eyes.

"It did," she said.

"How?" he asked.

"I'll explain it all later," she said.

Then she stood and stripped off her clothes as he watched intently. Quickly she was standing in front of him completely naked and enjoying his look.

All he could do was stare.

Finally he said, "You are so beautiful."

She imagined her hand firm and reached out for his hand.

"Come on," she said, actually feeling his hand solidly in hers as she pulled him to his feet. "We have some practicing to do."

"What kind of practicing?" he asked, smiling.

"The best kind," she said. "The very best."

And with that, Eve was convinced after just an hour of practice that they would live happily ever after together.

Only one small problem.

She was dead.

But it seemed that was a problem they could now live with.

Sample the Next Book

❦

THE DEEP SUNSET: A GHOST OF A CHANCE NOVEL

Chapter One

No one expects to die. Belle Watson sure didn't. Not on a beautiful November day in downtown Boise, Idaho.

Of course dying wouldn't have been any better on a crappy, rainy day, but this Wednesday afternoon was far, far from crappy. Clear blue fall sky, the leaves on the trees lining the sidewalks bright orange and red, and the afternoon temperature a perfect sixty-five, with no wind. Boise in early November, with the threat of winter right around the corner, didn't get much better, and that made dying just flat seem impossible, especially at the young and healthy age of twenty-eight.

No one dies while taking a day off work to just spend time with her best friend and do some clothes shopping. Not a high-risk kind of activity.

Belle felt and looked good, better than she had felt and

looked in years. She had dropped the thirty pounds she had gained from the eight-year horrid marriage to Brad Duncan, the high school quarterback who became the fat, sloppy, mean, self-proclaimed king of drunks.

He had seemed proud that he didn't work much and spent all his time in the Varsity Bar down off old Highway 99. He would see how proud he got when he didn't have her money so he could buy a drink.

She had only been in that bar once and had left in two minutes. It was dirty, smelled of piss and stale beer, and every surface she touched felt slimy. Yet her ex-husband had loved the place.

That alone showed how different they were.

The divorce had now been final for six months and Belle hadn't spoken with the slob in exactly six months.

And with luck, she never would again. To her friends and people at work she wouldn't even give him the title of her "ex-husband." To her he was just "the slug."

Now she had a brand new apartment in the beautiful, tree-lined streets of North End of town, with new furniture and a new red Mercedes convertible. She had also splurged on a brand new wardrobe that fit her thin, five-five frame perfectly and looked and was expensive. She didn't need to worry about money since she didn't need to support the slug anymore and had saved her mother's inheritance.

Besides, her job paid real nice as well. She had managed to finish college and get a masters degree in forensic accounting, marrying the slug as she finished the last of her thesis. Wow, what a mistake that had been. He couldn't even manage finishing two years of college. That should have been her first clue, but in those early years, he still looked like the football jock he had been in high school and could sweet-talk her out of her panties without a problem.

That part of their relationship had ended not long after they got married and she hadn't missed it in the slightest.

Now, on this beautiful afternoon, Belle hoped to improve the already expensive wardrobe some by adding in some fashionable winter clothes.

Belle had her long blonde hair pulled back and felt great walking the wide sidewalk down two blocks from the capital building, her low heals clicking on the pavement. She had been born and raised in Boise and had grown to love the downtown area with all its small shops, older buildings, and tree-lined sidewalks.

Strolling beside Belle was her long-time friend from high school, Nancy Bend. Nancy was also freshly out of a divorce from a worthless idiot who she had supported for years by working at a high-level development job at a start-up computer firm.

Belle and Nancy had gone to college and done their master's work at the same time. Nancy had her degrees in computer technology and could make any computer just get up off the desk and dance. What Nancy did for a job looked like magic to Belle. Nancy said what Belle understood about corporation financing and network systems was flat out magic period.

Nancy had caught the bastard she had been married to

sleeping with a waitress from Denny's where he spent most of his days drinking coffee and pretending to look for work.

Nancy hadn't talked to him either in five months, since the moment their divorce had been final. And Nancy had told Belle that sex with her husband had turned sour almost from the start and she didn't miss it either.

Belle and Nancy, after their divorces, had decided they needed to celebrate at least once a month, even though they spent a lot of time with each other normally, by taking a day off in the middle of the week, shopping, having a great dinner, going drinking, and otherwise just letting their hair down, so to speak.

Belle couldn't imagine the world without Nancy beside her. They spent most nights together having dinner and watching movies at one or the other's apartment.

Nancy was three inches taller than Belle, but just as thin. And Nancy also had money from the stock in the start-up firm she had been working at. Nancy had long brown hair that she usually kept up against the back of her head and large, green eyes that Belle loved.

And they made each other laugh. They had needed that laughter a lot over the last few years climbing out of those marriages. Luckily, for both of them, there were no kids involved. For Belle, the idea of having a kid with that slug of a human she had married made her just shudder.

Besides, she and the slug hadn't had sex in years and that had been just fine with her.

Belle and Nancy had been friends for so long, they basically did everything together. They had spent many a night drinking in the old Idanha Hotel luxury bar, laughing and holding each other while they cried and schemed during those years of first separation and then divorces.

And together, they had sworn off all men, which suited Belle just fine.

The November sky was clear, the weather warm, and they were shopping and laughing and enjoying life. Finally, for both of them, life was good again.

Dying was not in either of their plans for the day.

GHOST of a CHANCE

The DEEP SUNSET

DEAN WESLEY SMITH

Turn the Page to SAMPLE THE NEXT BOOK...

The Deep Sunset

CHAPTER ONE

No one expects to die. Belle Watson sure didn't. Not on a beautiful November day in downtown Boise, Idaho.

Of course dying wouldn't have been any better on a crappy, rainy day, but this Wednesday afternoon was far, far from crappy. Clear blue fall sky, the leaves on the trees lining the sidewalks bright orange and red, and the afternoon temperature a perfect sixty-five, with no wind. Boise in early November, with the threat of winter right around the corner, didn't get much better, and that made dying just flat seem impossible, especially at the young and healthy age of twenty-eight.

No one dies while taking a day off work to just spend time with her best friend and do some clothes shopping. Not a high-risk kind of activity.

Belle felt and looked good, better than she had felt and looked in years. She had dropped the thirty pounds she had gained from the eight-year horrid marriage to Brad Duncan, the high school quarterback who became the fat, sloppy, mean, self-proclaimed king of drunks.

He had seemed proud that he didn't work much and spent all his time in the Varsity Bar down off old Highway 99. He would see how proud he got when he didn't have her money so he could buy a drink.

She had only been in that bar once and had left in two minutes. It was dirty, smelled of piss and stale beer, and every surface she touched felt slimy. Yet her ex-husband had loved the place.

That alone showed how different they were.

The divorce had now been final for six months and Belle hadn't spoken with the slob in exactly six months.

And with luck, she never would again. To her friends and people at work she wouldn't even give him the title of her "ex-husband." To her he was just "the slug."

Now she had a brand new apartment in the beautiful, tree-lined streets of North End of town, with new furniture and a new red Mercedes convertible. She had also splurged on a brand new wardrobe that fit her thin, five-five frame perfectly and looked and was expensive. She didn't need to worry about money since she didn't need to support the slug anymore and had saved her mother's inheritance.

Besides, her job paid real nice as well. She had managed to finish college and get a masters degree in forensic accounting, marrying the slug as she finished the last of her thesis. Wow, what a mistake that had been. He couldn't even manage finishing two years of college. That should have been her first clue, but in those early years, he still looked like the football jock he had been in high school and could sweet-talk her out of her panties without a problem.

That part of their relationship had ended not long after they got married and she hadn't missed it in the slightest.

Now, on this beautiful afternoon, Belle hoped to improve the already expensive wardrobe some by adding in some fashionable winter clothes.

Belle had her long blonde hair pulled back and felt great walking the wide sidewalk down two blocks from the capital building, her low heals clicking on the pavement. She had been born and raised in Boise and had grown to love the downtown area with all its small shops, older buildings, and tree-lined sidewalks.

Strolling beside Belle was her long-time friend from high school, Nancy Bend. Nancy was also freshly out of a divorce from a worthless idiot who she had supported for years by working at a high-level development job at a start-up computer firm.

Belle and Nancy had gone to college and done their master's work at the same time. Nancy had her degrees in computer technology and could make any computer just get up off the desk and dance. What Nancy did for a job looked like magic to Belle. Nancy said what Belle understood about corporation financing and network systems was flat out magic period.

Nancy had caught the bastard she had been married to sleeping with a waitress from Denny's where he spent most of his days drinking coffee and pretending to look for work.

Nancy hadn't talked to him either in five months, since the moment their divorce had been final. And Nancy had told Belle that sex with her husband had turned sour almost from the start and she didn't miss it either.

Belle and Nancy, after their divorces, had decided they needed to celebrate at least once a month, even though they spent a lot of time with each other normally, by taking a day off in the middle of the week, shopping, having a great dinner, going drinking, and otherwise just letting their hair down, so to speak.

Belle couldn't imagine the world without Nancy beside her. They spent most nights together having dinner and watching movies at one or the other's apartment.

Nancy was three inches taller than Belle, but just as thin. And Nancy also had money from the stock in the start-up firm she had been working at. Nancy had long brown hair that she usually kept up against the back of her head and large, green eyes that Belle loved.

And they made each other laugh. They had needed that laughter a lot over the last few years climbing out of those marriages. Luckily, for both of them, there were no kids involved. For Belle, the idea of having a kid with that slug of a human she had married made her just shudder.

Besides, she and the slug hadn't had sex in years and that had been just fine with her.

Belle and Nancy had been friends for so long, they basically did everything together. They had spent many a night drinking in the old Idanha Hotel luxury bar, laughing and holding each other while they cried and schemed during those years of first separation and then divorces.

And together, they had sworn off all men, which suited Belle just fine.

The November sky was clear, the weather warm, and they were shopping and laughing and enjoying life. Finally, for both of them, life was good again.

Dying was not in either of their plans for the day.

Keep Reading *The Deep Sunset!*

Go to wmgbooks.com

Hear Directly from Dean

Receive exclusive content, keep up with the latest news, releases and so much more—even the occasional giveaway.

Go to deanwesleysmith.com.

Get the latest news and releases from all of the WMG authors and lines, including Dean Wesley Smith, *Pulphouse Fiction Magazine, Smith's Monthly,* and so much more.

Go to wmgbooks.com.

You can also follow Dean on Bookbub.

We value honest feedback, and would love to hear your opinion in a review, if you're so inclined, on your favorite book retailer's site.

Edited by Dean Wesley Smith

PULPHOUSE FICTION MAGAZINE

Pulphouse Fiction Magazine, edited by Dean Wesley Smith, made its return in 2018, twenty years after its last issue.

Each new issue contains about 70,000 words of short fiction. This reincarnation mixes some of the stories from the old *Pulphouse* days with brand-new fiction.

The magazine has an attitude, as did the first run. No genre limitations, but high-quality writing and strangeness.

Go to www.pulphousemagazine.com.

About the Author

DEAN WESLEY SMITH

Considered one of the most prolific writers working in modern fiction, with more than 30 million books sold, writer Dean Wesley Smith published far more than a hundred novels in forty years, and hundreds of short stories across many genres.

At the moment he produces novels in several major series, including the time travel Thunder Mountain novels set in the Old West, the galaxy-spanning Seeders Universe series, the urban fantasy Ghost of a Chance series, a superhero series starring Poker Boy, and a mystery series featuring the retired detectives of the Cold Poker Gang.

His monthly magazine, *Smith's Monthly*, which consists of only his own fiction, premiered in October 2013 and offers readers more than 70,000 words per issue, including a new and original novel every month.

During his career, Dean also wrote a couple dozen *Star Trek* novels, the only two original *Men in Black* novels, Spider-Man and X-Men novels, plus novels set in gaming and television worlds. Writing with his wife Kristine Kathryn Rusch under the name Kathryn Wesley, he wrote the novel for the

NBC miniseries The Tenth Kingdom and other books for *Hallmark Hall of Fame* movies.

He wrote novels under dozens of pen names in the worlds of comic books and movies, including novelizations of almost a dozen films, from *The Final Fantasy* to *Steel* to *Rundown*.

Dean also worked as a fiction editor off and on, starting at Pulphouse Publishing, then at *VB Tech Journal*, then Pocket Books, and now at WMG Publishing, where he and Kristine Kathryn Rusch serve as series editors for the acclaimed *Fiction River* anthology series.

For more information about Dean's books and ongoing projects, please visit his website at www.deanwesley-smith.com and sign up for his newsletter.

For more information:
www.deanwesleysmith.com

f facebook.com/deanwsmith3
P patreon.com/deanwesleysmith
BB bookbub.com/authors/dean-wesley-smith

Printed in the USA
CPSIA information can be obtained
at www.ICGtesting.com
CBHW011918270824
13785CB00010B/287